This book belongs to:

To Kate and Patrick for trusting me . . .
. . . and Mark for understanding my passion.

ORCHARD BOOKS

First published in Great Britain in 2015 by The Watts Publishing Group
This edition first published in 2016

1 3 5 7 9 10 8 6 4 2

Text © Mark Sperring, 2015
Illustrations © Mandy Sutcliffe, 2015

The moral rights of the author and illustrator have been asserted.

A CIP catalogue record for this book is available from the British Library.

ISBN 978 1 40833 709 7

Printed and bound in China

Orchard Books
An imprint of Hachette Children's Group
Part of The Watts Publishing Group Limited
Carmelite House
50 Victoria Embankment
London EC4Y 0DZ

An Hachette UK Company
www.hachette.co.uk

www.hachettechildrens.co.uk

Hop Along Boo

Along

Time For Bed

Mandy Sutcliffe

With words by Mark Sperring

ORCHARD

THE MOON PEEPS bright through the window.

The stars razzle-dazzle on high.

Boo, can you hear someone singing . . . ?

Belle's singing a lullaby!

She's strumming a sleepy old song now,

Singing, "Boo, it's time for your bed!"

So, Boo, don't you bunny around now.

The pillow's awaiting your head!

The whole world is snug in their jim-jams.
They've all brushed their teeth till they gleam.
They're all skipping out of the bathroom,
And heading off into a dream.

The cowboys way out on the prairie
Have wished all their horses goodnight.

They're climbing the stairs up to bed now,
While holding their teddy bears tight!

The dancers have hung up their shoes now.
Their pliés have all had to stop.

So, Boo, point your toes towards bed now,
And spring up those stairs with a hop!

The fairies, they flew up so sprightly,
Their wings glittered in the moon's glow . . .

. . . But the elephants thumped up like thunder.

I don't think they wanted to go!

All the babies are snug in their cots now,
As comfy as babies can be.
The toddlers have all toddled off now –
Just time for a story . . . or three!

All the big ships have dropped anchor – sploosh!

Little sailors are resting their heads.

Pirates are snoozing in hammocks.

Captain Boo, it's time for your bed!

So, Boo, there's no time for games now.
For most of the world's fast asleep.
And Belle's little song has turned into a . . .

. . . YAAAAAAAAAAAWN!

So hop to it, Boo.

Move those feet!

Bedtime and blankets are waiting.
Cuddles and snuggles are too.

On a pillow as soft as a feather,

Let's whisper . . .

. . . "Goodnight, Belle and Boo."

The moon peeps bright
through the window.

The stars razzle-dazzle
on high . . .

Join Belle and her bunny, Boo, on a
dreamy adventure, meeting many
friends along the way . . .

Take your little one
on a lullaby journey,
ending in a perfect
night's sleep.

www.belleandboo.com

LOVE STORIES, LOVE ORCHARD

ISBN 978-1-40833-709-7

£6.99

9 781408 337097

orchardbooks.co.uk